KARA'S DREAMS

Story by RITU ANAND
Illustrations by VEEN REDWOOD

PathBinder
Publishing

COLUMBUS,
INDIANA

KARA'S DREAMS

Story by RITU ANAND

Illustrations by VEEN REDWOOD

Published by PathBinder Publishing
P.O. Box 2611
Columbus, IN 47202
www.PathBinderPublishing.com

Illustrations and covers designed by Veen Redwood
Interior and back cover text formatted by Anna Perlich

First published in 2022

Manufactured in the United States

ISBN 978-1-955088-09-1
Library of Congress Control Number: 2021925574

To Sri Guru Granth Sahibjee:

Thank you for your guidance.

To the late Sri Joginder Singh Anand: Rest in Peace.

Thank you Daddy for being a quiet role model and for

showing me the way to appreciate nature.

To students of Visible Men Academy:

May all your dreams come true.

To my dear husband Hon. Harry Anand:

Thank you for your support.

Foreword

Some years ago, when I was teaching fourth grade, I had a conversation with a fifth-grade teacher of ours about doing a great, big project with our students. We were beginning a long, arduous year preparing our boys for state tests. In truth, we had not looked forward to them at all; we knew that, though important, state tests could never measure our students' academic growth or capture the full breadth of our students' potential—their strengths, gifts, and talents. A few students would surely excel, but most of them who started the year two or three years below grade level (some even speaking no English) would never get the opportunity to show just how much they knew and how much they had learned.

Secretly, tentatively, and excitedly, we began to contemplate the possibility of doing some plays with our "Suns." By January of that school year, some months before entering the dreaded testing period, we were teaching our students about Shakespeare. We collaborated in the afternoons, combining our classes, so they could learn about the elements of theater, including learning to read and understand scripts, acting out scenes, creating 3D models of the Globe Theatre, and practicing reading sonnets. We even decided to read a novel called The Shakespeare Stealer to get our students excited about bringing Shakespeare's plays to life. Though we knew our vision for this project was a meaningful one, we were also worried about preparing our students for their state tests. We didn't know it then, but if there were any reservations about doing Shakespeare plays with our students, one of our school volunteers was going to put them to rest.

Ms. Ritu, as we and our students affectionately call her, had been volunteering at our school, working with students individually and sometimes in groups. I still remember so vividly the sparkle in her eyes when she first met my students. She could hardly contain her smile and excitement that students and teachers alike welcomed her and treated her as if she had been a member of our school community for years. My students looked forward to seeing her whenever she came. They especially loved the fact that she would bring books and read stories to them. Little by little, my coworker and I began to include Ms. Ritu in our conversations about Shakespeare. And seemingly all at once, she had convinced us that doing Shakespeare with our students was most certainly a worthwhile endeavor and one she would be happy and eager to dedicate time to.

By far, one of the greatest privileges and honors I have had in my life is to have worked on that project with my former coworker and Ms. Ritu. It was an absolute success and remains the highlight of my teaching career. Our students not only performed A Midsummer Night's Dream and Hamlet, but they also recited a dozen sonnets and performed two songs with the help of Key Chorale, a symphonic chorus based in Sarasota, Florida. Ms. Ritu was not only responsible for helping our students memorize lines, sonnets, movements, and gestures; she was instrumental in helping us realize our vision. Where we failed to reach students, she spoke words that led them to believe in themselves.

Because our students come from disenfranchised, low-income communities, we know that stress, adversity, trauma, pain, and suffering are things they often must endure daily. As such, in working with these students—mostly boys of color—there is heartbreak daily. The effect this has on some people is that it leads them to place limitations on our students. And yet, heartbreak is not what moved us to believe they could learn, read, and perform Shakespeare at the fourth- and fifth-grade levels. Nor was it sympathy. It was the unwavering belief that they have beautiful gifts to offer to this world and that they deserve a place and an environment where these gifts can emerge and flourish. It was the shared understanding that if we can teach them to stand tall even in the face of difficulties, they can and will find the strength to fight their way through any seemingly insurmountable deficits and develop the courage to pursue their dreams.

That is a message that Ms. Ritu has conveyed to every one of our students. It is the message she has gifted to every student she has ever worked with at Visible Men Academy. And it is the message she conveys in the beautifully written story of Kara's Dreams. At a time when we are still suffering and recovering from the repercussions of a worldwide pandemic, Kara's Dreams has the power to resonate with young readers who may find themselves behind in school and in life. It could not be timelier, as the wisdom of this story lies in the things it teaches them and us about resilience, perseverance, compassion, and relentless optimism. These are among the most noble of human attributes. They do not only define our humanity, but also uplift it.

I am grateful for Ms. Ritu and for her beautiful story. It has been crafted with thought, care, and love. It will certainly have a place in the collection of stories I share with my students when I speak to them about our school values and principles. It will inspire them as well as those beyond Visible Men Academy to be strong, to stand tall, and to be visible.

—Diego Velasco

Dean of Students at Visible Men Academy, Bradenton, Florida

Kara dreamed of growing as tall and strong as Utsa.

Utsa had been standing tall for more than two hundred years.

But ...

Kara had many fears.

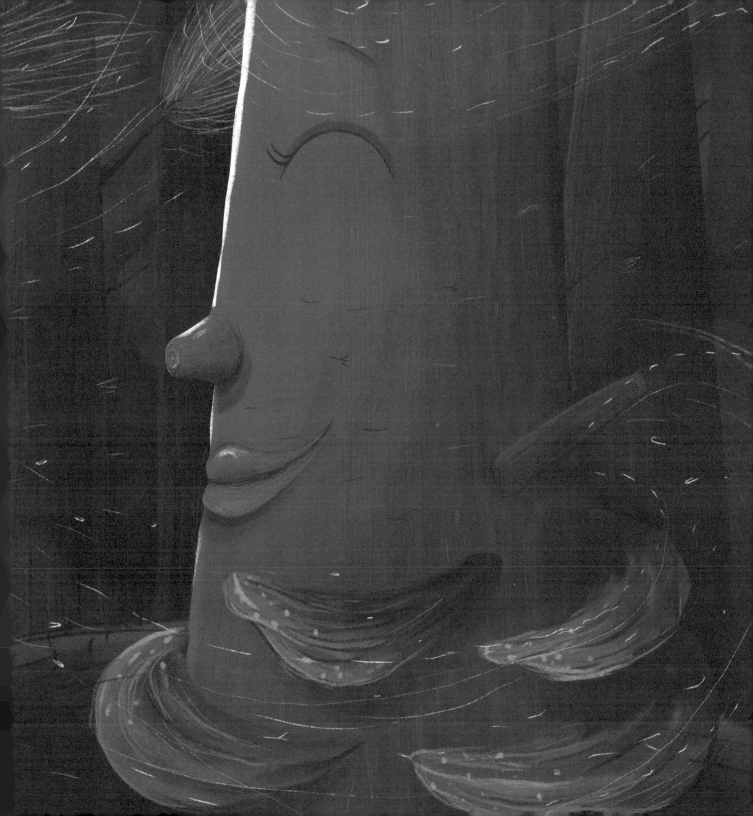

She feared Wind could smash her,
Water could drench her,
Earth could swallow her,
And Night, cold and dark, could freeze her

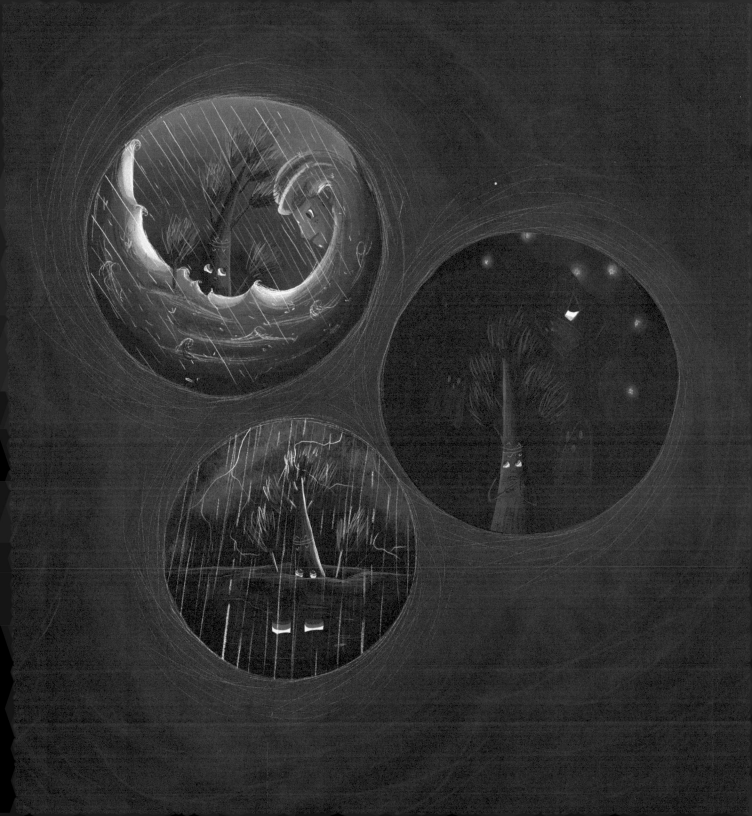

Some days, Kara woke up and found her friends swaying in the breeze.

Other days, she heard Wind crack and snap some of them to the ground.

One stormy night, Kara's leaves quivered in the rain.

"Could I be fearless?" she wondered.

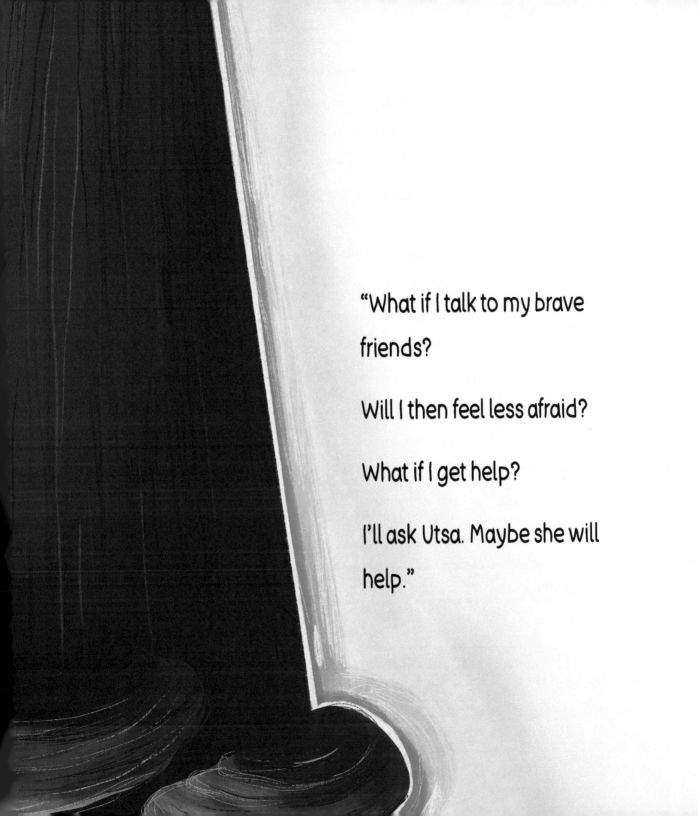

"What if I talk to my brave friends?

Will I then feel less afraid?

What if I get help?

I'll ask Utsa. Maybe she will help."

"Hello, Utsa. How have you held up high for so long?

Do you have a secret magic or a super power?" Kara asked.

"Dear Kara, let me tell you this story about Aa-hum and Viheen from when they were growing up," Utsa replied.

Utsa continued. "One night, a hurricane hit the forest. Many trees fell.

Aa-hum listened to howling Wind and swung with her. Swish! Swish! Swish!

Viheen threw sharp needles at Wind.

"Heavy rain poured onto Aa-hum, and she took it as if she were taking a shower.

Viheen smirked at Water.

Earth started washing away, but
Aa-hum dug her roots deep to
embrace her like her own Mother.

Viheen shook his roots instead.

He sneered at Night, while Aa-hum
huddled with Night.

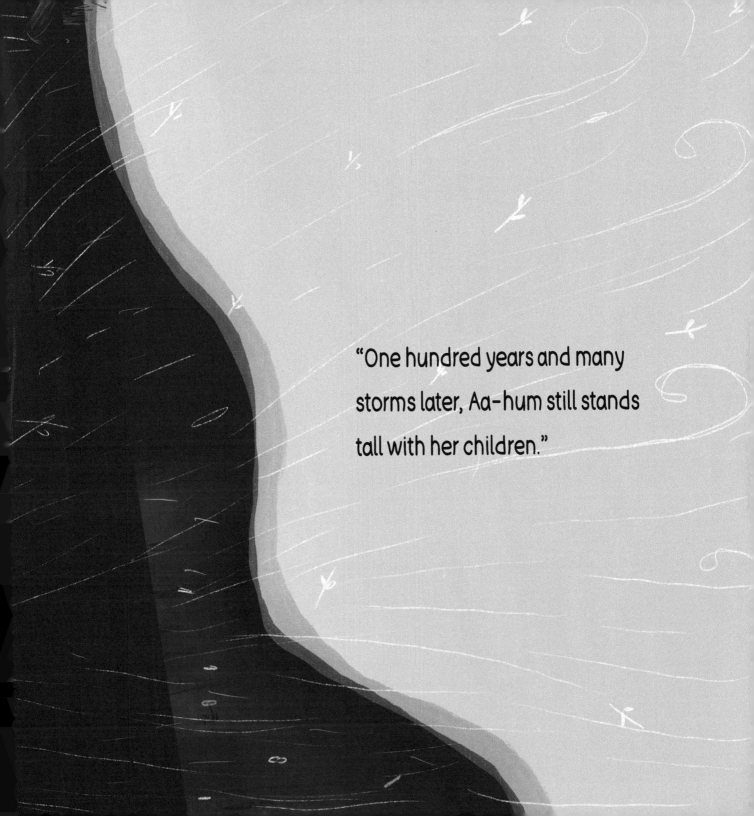

"One hundred years and many storms later, Aa-hum still stands tall with her children."

"What happened to Viheen?" Kara asked.

"Wind shattered him to pieces. One wounded part lies next to you," Utsa answered.

Kara wondered and wanted to know, so she asked Utsa, "Have you ever felt nervous?"

Utsa replied, "I certainly have. It was the first gusty night for my daughter, Aa-hum, and her cousin, Viheen. I was worried for their safety."

"Hmm ..." Kara said to herself.

"If I just smile and believe all is well, all will be well," said Kara.

That night, Wind charged at Kara.

Kara smiled and bowed as Wind passed by.

Water slammed, and Kara's roots drank all they could.

As Earth slipped and slid, Kara dug deep and hugged Mother, pulling her closer.

Night cradled her and soon turned into Day.

Day welcomed chirps, tweets, whistles, and a symphony of songs by songbirds.

One tune touched a chord in Kara, and soft Wind breezed through her.

Kara stretched tall and said
with conviction:

"I will hum through storms.

I will dance to tunes.

I will reach my dreams."

About the Author

Ritu Anand started writing when she could hold a pencil, but life kept getting in the way. For the past four years, she has chosen Writing as her career. She draws her inspiration from nature around her and her scripture – Sri Guru Granth Sahibjee.

When she sat down to write *Kara's Dreams,* her pen flowed its ink onto paper, as a river floods its banks. The beautiful verse within the scripture that guided her story provides – Pavan Guru, Paani Pita, Mata Dharadh Mahat, Divas Raat Duii Dayee Daya, Khaileh Sagal Jagat. It means the Wind is the Guru. Water is the Father. Earth is the Mother. Day and Night are caretakers. All the elements – Wind, Water, Earth, Night and Day work in concert to enable creatures to play and enjoy this playground called Earth.

Ritu Anand lives in Sarasota, Florida with her loving husband. Her interests include reading, writing, singing Indian classical music, dancing to Bollywood music, traveling and playing golf.

About the Illustrator

Veen Redwood has been a full-time children's book illustrator since 2019. Because she never stopped believing in magic, her mind is filled with a sense of curiosity about and an enthusiasm for the world of fantasy. She strongly believes she can bring the words of a story to life through illustrations using the magic in her hands. *Kara's Dreams* is her nineteenth book.

Visit us at www.PathBinderPublishing.com

This title is available in hardback, paperback and e-book

CPSIA information can be obtained
at www.ICGtesting.com
Printed in the USA
LVHW071314050422
715343LV00008B/204